The Whisper Behind
The Wind

. . . always there
we know it in our bones
deny it to our hearts.

The Whisper Behind The Wind

Poems by

Walkin' Jim Stoltz

Best Wishes Kathleen

Walkin Jim Stoltz

11-3-95

Lone Coyote Publications 1988

My thanks to my partner, Leslie,
and all the folks on the road who
encouraged me to publish this collection.

Copyright © 1988 by Walkin' Jim Stoltz
All rights reserved
Printed in Bozeman, Montana
United States of America
First Edition
ISBN 0-9620228-0-2
Lone Coyote Publications
Box 477
Big Sky, MT 59716

For my Mother
and the Earth,
One and the same.

The Poems

The River

There's a river flowing through me,

It sings a wild tune

And murmurs secrets to the winds,

Blows free through the canyons in my dreams.

Flowing

And flowing clean

Dancing free as Time itself,

Bleeding tears surging from the Earth

Rising now in song

Wrung from the mountain's heart,

Dripping from the forest's breath

Rushing to flood.

A glimpse of the newborn,

A nod to the Old,

A vision

Of the river

Dammed inside us all

Breaking free

To sing again.

A Coyote Answers, "Brother"

On nights when the moon is full
  expecting
When dewy silver coats each scrubby pine
  and grassy meadow
When mountains kiss passion
  in embrace for the night
I step to a rhythm
  outside my own
And roam quietly
  back
To something we all once had
Something lost to us
  in the standing
  in glossing over and paving under
  in turning away blind to the past
   and rootless tomorrow.

It comes back

Back, under cover of dark

  with the flow of moonbeams

Falling on tangled hair, wet grass

  and pine needles

Stalking silence, as I

On lion's feet

Curious to be alive

Moving now

Can't hold back this joy

This old song, reborn

Given back

Flowing from surging wells

It springs forth

From marrow to blood

  From soul to spirit

    From heart to voice

To song I howl!

The Earth swallows the sound

Wind carrying away the crumbs,

But somewhere

Over the ridge

Oh, so faintly

A coyote answers, "Brother."

Mountain Moment

Ho! Great sleeper

Child of fire

Prodigy of essence,

You who rest wisdom

Caressed from glaciers

Molded through the wind

Given back.

You are the Mountain.

You are the Heart.

Power calling

Living rock

Rooted to the mantle

Based in the core

Shining to sky-kissed clouds

These are times I need that power,

Times I come

Calling, searching your reality

For my own.

Vigil

From the Ruby Range
I followed the sun
First, being eaten by glowing aspen
Then, devoured by gold desert soil
Soaking up the last light
Like water spilled haphazard
Sucked up by thirsting sage.

Heat still breathed
In the big rocks, living.
I joined their vigil
Silent and still
A witness
Eyes and ears, content
To be part stone.

The bird landed on my shoulder
Looking for a warm perch.
My soft landing questioned her,
Tilted head
Puzzling at my ear.
Those seconds were mine,
The rock in me
Coming home,
Granite patience
Gently flying to the air world,
Fragile wild heart
Touching mine, buried deep.
She flew off into the twilight;
I reached up and caressed my shoulder.

The Drawings

I came down the canyon
Searching water,
A cool place to hide from the sun,
Softly, for the silence was old
And deep
On watch-for-all feet.

I found the seep, but kept on,
Twisting narrows
Sirens call
Answering just around the bend.
The cave waited.
I ran up the tilted slab
The rock, cool under my fingers
And under the canyon wall
The air stale and dust deep
Powder rising from each step
What place is this?
Walls covered with dancing herds of bighorn
Leaping deer and spread-eagled men,
Ceiling men of flying, snake bodies
Fresh this day
As it was those thousand years past.
I glanced over my shoulder
Half seeing
Chanting shaman
Barefoot prints
Faces 'round a living fire.

I left
Shaking chills off my spine
But came back later
To sleep and dream.

Of Knowledge

Knowledge, born of feeling
        a circle of sense.
Words have no lesson half as strong
        as a mountain mile.
Feeling through
        that extra sense
The heart,
Earth sings clear
        if we Listen with more than ears,
Season shares secrets
        if we Open more than eyes,
Self finds the Way
        if we Feel
        rather than think.

True knowledge roots within
Webbed strands
Ties to all.
Earth sings to season
Season shares the Way
And Self finds Earth
        Again
        And again.

Bridge

I met a man

In the reflection of a child

Face to face,

Eye to eye

Halfway across the old swinging bridge,

In the mirror

Of a dusky river.

I smiled in recognition

He smiled back

Knowing where it was

Our paths had crossed before

And why.

Home
for Leslie

Like the young river

I have flowed

Through the mountain's breach

And forest's sweep,

I have rolled my waters

Through the lives

Of searching eyes

And hearts

But found no home

No safe place to rest

No warm place to grow

Until I touched your

Shining shore.

Heart songs sing

Together,

Bound in love

For Love.

For all roots are homed in love

And in loving,

We know

We are truly Home.

Old One

Old One, wind-rider

Stalks crimson sunsets

Canyon silence

Stillness of the narrows,

Walks today

Searching remnants

Matching spirit

Knowing.

Old One,

I feel you in these

    windswept lonely places

In the calm of

    breathless echoes.

Your touch lies

Gentle on the land

Steps still sound

    in shadow of the ledges

    the far side of golden mesas.

Earth holds you

Spirit whole

Knowing.

Old one

Come walk

With this wayward disciple.

I feel you

But know you only

In songs left hanging

In the desert night

The coyote cry,

Spirit flight.

Come walk,

Steps you've known.

Vision

To Vision

We crawl.

Bull River Woods

The sun
Jilted thief
Sneaking in where it can
Stealing from the cool shade
Dew drops perpetual home
Earth moist and giving footfalls silent
Foot-deep needle carpet and
Moss like sponge, springing back

Green is breathable essence
More than color
Wrung from feathered ferns
And rolled to giant's canopy
Fluid spectrum catching vitality
In one seed
Bloomed to colossal monuments
Arms unable to skirt their girth
Even five times 'round,
Though to embrace
Gives back

Living being, there is wisdom here
Age rippling bark
Solemn green energy
Proud source
How can it be?
There are those who walk here
With stacked lumber in their eyes
And dollar-signs on their lips.

Bristlecone

I have seen you

Clutching for life

Perched atop the rocky craig

And open ridge

Windblown for centuries

Of snow blasts and icy gales,

You know them all.

Twisted in your youth

You've grown wild

Whichever way the mountain moves you;

Years mean so little

Waiting at 11,000 feet

High above the last of the others.

It's as if you know

What fate lies below;

Better to rub shoulders with the wind

Chanting wisdom to Time

Narrows

The silence here is that of sleep,

Bare rock, smooth and sheer

      bears lines of sleep

Time stands in the stillness

It soothes and stirs

A mix of calm

      and the promised rush.

This is from another Age

      a world of its own

Humankind has no place here

      their time no meaning,

Water rules here

      even when it's gone

Its presence runs with the twist of the canyon

      the polished rock

      the tubs of stone.

I am but a visitor

Like the deer come to gawk

I feel the time in this place

      it weighs heavy on mortal shoulders

I taste the beauty

      it lightens my heart

I feel the silence

      the stillness and calm

That rings of peace.

The Flute

I used to carry my flute
Smooth bamboo, unsheathed and ready
Through the hollows
Searching out those perfect echoes

But grew tired of the grip
Tenuous and sweaty
It slipped to the loop at my hip
Close at hand, by my side

The places of Sound
Were dying, even then
The notes found flight
Easier than living on

I swapped it for a guitar
And searched for words
Tunes hiding in living dreams
Tossing the flute back to the rising flood.

And Death Danced With Life

That wisdom of the Earth

Breeds deep reflection

In each face I gaze upon,

The mountain knows in its waiting

The river rises to the knowledge

Horsetails sweep the sand,

    a hieroglyphic message

    left to the day.

The pika runs frantic amid the rocks,

    sure of what's to come

They know

In life, and living

In Death, and dying

    They know.

I came upon a pigmy owl flapping wildly

A splash of life on the dead snow,

The woodpecker in her clutches

    beneath her, gave a cry,

Owl eyes

Piercing, wild through me

Dared to take that food away

Yellow orbs mesmerized

And I stood in the cold, mouth agape,

Watching the great book unfold

    Another page.

Then,

Feathers flew

A flowing vitality,

Spirit living

Survive, both hearts cried!

Survive, both beaks screamed!

Blood, blinding bright and rich red

      stained the snow

      soaking deeper to a lush rose

And Death danced with Life

Each bird crying

      let me live.

She let go her prey

And flew to a low perch a few yards away,

The air was charged

Itself, a living thing

Each moment nudged the next minute to move

Woodpecker, bloodied and crazed

      writhed silent in tracks of struggle

And then

With purpose

Limped and tottered toward her,

She who would live, today

An offering

A giving

A blessing of Death to Life

They know.

The owl stretched her head skyward

Then swooped to take her meal.

Survival

A worm leads a sheltered life
Crawling in and out,
Hiding from a shovel's slash
And leaving no doubt,
That he'd rather stay right there
    where he was
Than be swallowed by a trout.

Still On The Run

I have found the magic of the wild

Tasted the vitality of the untamed,

For this is true freedom.

It flows from the heart

Uncaged, and strong

A rich essence

Rooted in the living Earth,

Flowering in each individual being,

And touching home

In me.

For there is a freedom there

A spirit that flows with the clear mountain streams

Blows through the virgin spruce

And cries with the call of the eagle.

It's a part of all who have been

And all who will be,

A part of the Earth

A part of the wind, the water

A part of Us

It roams ever free

Sings ever wild,

That spirit is

Still on the run

Bat Cave

In the full heat of mid-day
Waiting in the brushed wall of the canyon
I found the cave
Proud of my direction
Water dripped, somewhere
In the cool dark
I wetted my cracked lips
Trying hard to swallow
Ginger steps of brail
Feeling toward that sound
Willing eyes to penetrate the void.

That's when the cave came to life
Walls waving to a hum of nervous wings
Ceiling, a threat of bursting thousands
To fly away
Whirring,
Those waiting
Moving masses
Like a sound track to a scarey movie
Chilling hair stood on end
As I suddenly remembered
I could probably go a while yet
Without the water.

Rainbow Trails

I walk the rainbow trails

High and rolling

Open to whatever pots of gold

These days may bring,

I feast on dusty plains

Borrow time from desert mornings

And lean on mountain winds

Drawing closer

With each passing mile

A constant search for color

Along the trails

Within myself.

Powerpoint-Schell Creek Range

The snow at 10,000 feet
A sleeping giant nestled tight
In the mountain's fold
Squeezing, bear-hug grip on Spring
Loathe to wake and move on
Down
To the desert.

I kicked my steps
A steady give and take
Patient with streaming sun
And post-holed miles
Bristlecone and limber pines waving
Distorted arms, polished trunks glistening
Twisted wood reaching to the past
Haunting hands stretched to today.

It had snowed an hour before
Fresh flurries hiding on the season's tally
Huddling in the crooks of every tree
Hungry for the kiss of shale
Masking clouds dressing like Iowa.
Now the sun owned this range
And me, slogging along the ridge
Content to call out to soaring ravens
To caress weathered pines
To catch in one glance hundreds of square miles
Far-off snow covered range, upon range
To kick my freezing toes home
Again and again.

Deer-worn tracks

Beaten through the snow a hundred times

Up and over the crest

Rabbit, lynx, and squirrels

Had left their sign, a claim -

      "This is wild country."

My kind visit here but seldom

Searching prospects, answers hidden on the wind

Or engrained in the contour

      of a weathered pine

      of a flowing mountain

There is power here

My heart feels it

Spirit welcoming it, homecoming

Reaching to an age outside

      Way out there

Embracing the mountain's course

Content to lie with the snow

And follow it 'round

From sleeping ridge to awakening desert

Again and again

For an eon

There is strength

In giving to the mountain.

There is hope

In reaching back

To time.

I slid down, into the pass
On my fanny
Out of control and scared
Loving the letting go
Fearing the mountain's hand
Trusting snowy palms.
On dry ground I rolled to my feet
In a circle of bare Earth, medicine wheel?
Four feet across, laced in piled snow
Standing island, sanctuary
Paws feeling firm
Rooted to the grass and dirt,
My hand reached
Out of its own, beyond thought
And in my grip
A piece of stone
Tool, chipped to perfection
White as bleached bone
Perched for all time
Waiting?
Vision reeled in colors of strength and hope
Tears streamed weighted in power
I squeezed it to the sky.

The Hunters

The car leaves the 7-11

On first light fuel

Stale donuts and black coffee

Armed with six-packs of skunky,

      piss-water beer - Coors

Wives and kids left behind

So they can

Feel their balls and swing their guns

And tell themselves lies

How hard it was to blow an elk away

At thirty yards

With an M-16.

The lioness stalked patience

For an hour

Rushed like flood

Into the herd when they caught her scent

Elk spilling over the sides of the bowl

Crying hooves, singing dirge

She was fast

Dashing flesh, claws ripping

Dive into the old cows haunches

They go down together

Blood screaming

Bones cracking.

Green and Growing

Earth wisdom

Speaks in green

And sings in growing,

It stands in Life

Both feet firm to the ground

Roots to the flowing river

Eye to eye with the sacred source.

Destined to air

  Born of water

    Child of Earth

Bound to flower even in deathsong,

Strong and sure woody hearts

Are born to bend and dance

To bear seeds of light

To carry on

A legacy

Of green and growing.

Forest

I come back

Hiding in your arms

Crying on your shoulder,

Soaking my roots

With yours

For just one moment

Takes me home.

Joshua Tree

Desert morning limps along
Dry, heat waves across the plain
Stillness catches hold and squeezes

Distant visage
Spokes of green
Trees? Here?

Closer now
Splayed stalks of spiked fronds
Trunks, bowed and twisted
Bobbing snakeheads out reaching for what?
Shall I even call them trees?

Thin shade, but deep
To hide from the relentless one
A breather to pause
Letting the sweat dry
Listening
To marvel at one forest
Safe from the logger's saw.

Aspen Graffiti
(Wasatch Plateau)

Light plays easy games

Darting in dancing leaves

Smooth silver trunks

Beaver's feast, soft bark

Yearning for a touch

Just so.

Eighty-year-old scars,

"July 9 - 1907"

Stretched gray deadwood

Living graffiti,

Bored sheepmen's favorite passtime

It seems.

Here, an '08

There, a 1912

And there's an '01.

Unpronounced names

Letters grown into years,

Food for educated shaking leaves

Full-blown portraits, tree art

Mountains, elk, naked forms of

man and woman

And there ...

My, how those fellows liked their sheep.

Windsinger Mountain

I

Mountain peaks
Are for dreamers
Visions, on eagle wings
Whisper behind the wind
Falling to seed
Echoing in vastness
Of Spirit
Flowing now
Alive forever.

II

Summit cairn, alter
To the miles
Lifelines to eternity
Of mountain, after mountain
Untouched
A pearl of primitive
Still whole and breathing wild,
And of valley upon valley
Checkerboarded, crossed by roads
Powerlines, like giant insects feeding
Chopped into fine pieces, dying.
Windsingser -
Symphonies born now
Of Earth and Air
Of tributes, resounding
Odes of lament
Echoes of the past.

The Birth

Rising up, the bushes rattle
A dozen partridge
Launched to the sky.

Ripples, outward wave
Shining truth
Bound for the grave.

Words dropped so
On tiny seeds
Waiting for the rain.

Wolf

Wolf, where have we sent you?

Limping, one leg shot

Hanging from meat hooks in the trees

Poisoned with your kin

Skinned and left to rot

Under skies

Of justice?

Your song still echoes

On dying winds

In mountains patched with islands

Still living whole and wild

In plains fenced and tamed

In the far reaches

Within us all

Rooted to the Earth

Yet, unknown to it.

Wolf,

When will my brothers cry

And sisters weep

For your green fire

And streaming blood

Spilled from their own hearts?

Rock Dream

Shaded from the sun

I took welcome shelter

Under the ledge.

The dark slot in the smooth wall

Gaped like a giant's grin

And swallowed me whole.

When night came I stretched out

Under the rock,

The sandstone a few feet above my face,

And wondered when this shoulder would shrug,

Rock crashing down

Taking me back in one pulverizing smash.

I could feel it there

Pressing down upon me,

Compressing my bones to fossil,

Dashing my brains to powdery dust

And blood oozing with the stone seams

From that moment, forever

Destined to dream of rock,

My epitaph sleeping

In the smooth canyon wall.

Requiem to a Coon

The coon begins to roam with the fall of night
Scurrying after curiosity's questioned sight,
Down to the dump to scour the cans,
Scrounge the trash, garbage of man,
The campgrounds, over the hill on a run
Dodging the beams of flashlight guns,
He scats to a dirty pan of bacon fat,
Freezing to a camper's, "what's that?"
Then off to the highway to visit the bones
Of a neighbor or two who never came home,
Waiting for headlights to die in the night
Making the crossing in habitual rite.
Down the ravine through briars and brambles
Loping his way on his evening ramble,
The river meets him with a splash
Wading in to find his stash,
He drags out a clam, fresh and cold
And cracks it on a rock, meat unfolds.
Along the banks he stalks the water's purr
When the night is broken with a cry,
        the flash of steel, the bite of fur!
Trapped! To slowly die in an iron grasp
Squeezing the color from his wide-eyed mask.
Clamped jaws incase his paw in fire,
Each movement pulls and strains, he begins to tire.
Then, knowing it vain to tug at the biting claws
He sees freedom in his own needle sharp jaws
And attacks the leg with escape in mind,
Tearing flesh and bone in a rage full blind,
His own blood filling his mouth, staining his teeth,
And at last limping away three legs free.

A grub of a man came by
In the morning of the next day,
Meeting the sight of a gristled, fly covered paw
With only two words to say,
"Got away."

Lone Mountain

(Madison Range, Montana)

In the sleepy hours, awakening
I saw you rising, coming whole
Clouds lacing your feet
And kissing your brow like feathers.

You'll make your own fluffy whites
In time to meet the wind
Tossing to the sun
More than you'll ever get back.

The cannons throw shells at you
Gnats buzzing to your skin
Come, shake these pests
Go back to your quiet mountain dreams.

Earth Mother

I have seen you
Naked in the morning
Calling out to me.

There in full bloom
Color for the heart
Seeds bearing Light.

I have felt you
Open and giving
Anchoring roots and singing fruit.

But who will hear you
Weeping for the Dark
Dying for a listen?

Track

Bit by bit
Water kisses the track,
Seeping mud print, oozing and shiny
Pads and claws clear
Reaching rich
Stretching untamed.

Frozen, fresh track marks time
Like the wild land itself,
Calling to today
And a thousand yesterdays
To something in me,
Deep within
Caged in my own tracks.

Instinct demands a wary glance behind
To the side and about
Bear smell lingers.
I stoop to the dirt
Entranced in perfect lines,
Each nuance of the great paw
Ingrained in the living Earth
And me.

I feel it touching

But can't understand where.

Is it the untamed singing in my soul?

The wild spirit playing to my heart?

Or is it

The unbridled fear tossing

in my gut?

Bushes rustle,

My stomach flops.

I'll not stop for answers now.

My tracks

I leave with grizz,

A question mark on any trail

To be swallowed by the Earth

And eaten by the wind.

My Guitar

for Stella

You walked with me longer than anyone
Catching tunes from the mountain wind
And in the soft lonesome, sage-covered plains,
Finding music in the sweep of wild desert
Or the deep forests of your fathers
And giving it all to me.

I carried you on my back
Knowing you would never search out these places
      on your own,
You were an outsider, more than I
But you loved it, and thrived.
You took more beatings than I ever could
Bleaching your hide blond in the sun
Freezing your crumbling finish in the snows
Cracking your wooden bones each time I
      stumbled and fell,
But always there to sing a song.

The age on your face
Was miles we'd walked.
The tune on your strings,
The heart of what we found.

You saved my life one sunny day
Falling down a Utah ice field,
Digging in your heels
Just in time,
The cliff below had tried to claim me
But you cried, "Oh no, not yet!"

Yes, and you gave me back my life

Each time I strummed your weathered skin

Each time I held you

And gave my voice

To yours

Each time you showed me something

Old or new.

Today I nod my head to you

Hanging on the wall

Gathering dust, waiting

And know you'll be there

Always singing

And wondering if I would ever dare

Turn you into a planter.

No Trail's End

I have walked too many trails,
Too many dusty roads
I call home.
The blistering sun and freezing cold
Have left their claw-like scars upon my hide,
Skin aging so much faster than my heart.
Yet, I know
I will go again.
An empty desert valley will call me out
As a distant blue
Mountain range will draw me in.
A hidden canyon, turning unknown corners
Will beg me to follow
While a forest path will lead me
Back, to where I need to be.
These,
These are my places
Of power.
I seem to be a better man
In the wilds,
More whole, more complete
More atune
More me.
I have said many times
There is a magic there,
And there is.
But it lies not only
In the special magic
Of the Earth,
The wind songs and the sun,
But also
In me.

This is a magic not hoarded
Or chained in secrecy
But a spirit shared by all
Life, and all eternity.
It binds me to the Mother,
The creatures of my dreams
And the sleeping singers,
The mountain and the plain.
This bond
It draws me
Into myself, and yet also
To the root
Of this great tree
I am a part of.
My power comes from knowing things
Perhaps not in words,
But in feelings
Touching back
To the Earth, growing
To other ages, living
To distant lives, blooming
All next to mine.

Yes, I will go again
When that bond is buried
In the roar of Man
In the scream of so-called progress
In my own blindness.
I will go again
For there is no trail's end
I have walked too many trails.

About the Author

Walkin'Jim Stoltz has walked well over 15,000 miles through the backcountry of America in the past 14 years. Each year he puts on his walkin' shoes, ties his guitar, Stella, onto his pack, and heads out into the wilderness. During his long, solo walks Jim soaks up the magic of those wild places. It comes out in each story, poem, and song. He has recorded two albums of his songs, *Spirit Is Still On The Run* and *Forever Wild*, and travels extensively when not on the trail, playing for audiences from coast to coast. He currently resides in Big Sky, Montana with his wife, Leslie.

Walkin' Jim's two albums, *Spirit Is Still On The Run* and *Forever Wild* are available for $11 each (includes postage) in record or cassette, from:

Lone Coyote Records
Box 477
Big Sky, MT 59716

If you would like to be on our mailing list for future books or recordings, please send us your name and address.